WITCH WAY TO THE COUNTRY

WITCH WAY
TO THE COUNTRY

Barbara Mariconda

illustrated by
Jon McIntosh

A Yearling First Choice Chapter Book

For Jim and Pat Giff
—B.M.

For Tip and Jack
—J.M.

Published by
Bantam Doubleday Dell Publishing Group, Inc.
1540 Broadway
New York, New York 10036

Cataloging-in-Publication Data is available from the U.S. Library of Congress
ISBN 0-385-32179-1 (hardcover); ISBN 0-440-41100-9 (paperback)

The text of this book is set in 17-point Baskerville.
Manufactured in the United States of America
October 1996
10   9   8   7   6   5   4   3   2   1

CONTENTS

1.
READY, SET, GO!

"It's that time of year," said Drusilla
to her cat, Hiss.
"Time to see my
country cousin Constance!
Time to go to the country fair!"
Drusilla and Hiss packed their things.
Drusilla hummed.
Hiss hissed.

"Time to start up the vacuum,"
said Drusilla.
Whoosh, went the vacuum.
It started right up.
That was the good news.
The bad news was that
Hiss was in the way.
"Look out for your tail!"
yelled Drusilla.

But it was too late.

Hiss had a hairless tail.

"That's okay," said Drusilla.

"It will grow back."

"Hiss!" said hairless Hiss.

They hopped on the vacuum.

Off they flew over the city.

"Country Cousin, here I come,"
sang Drusilla.

"Goodbye traffic!" she yelled.

"Goodbye skyscrapers!" she said.

"Goodbye subways!" she called.

"Goodbye pigeons!" she added.

Hiss hissed.

Higher and higher they flew.

"Hold on to your hat!"

shouted Drusilla.

Hiss held on to his hat.
That was the good news.
The bad news was that he
was the only one who did.

2.
COUNTRY COUSIN CONSTANCE

"It's that time of year," said Constance
to her mynah bird, Myrna.
"Time for the country fair!"
"But first I must clean
the cottage!"

Constance started right up.

She cleaned her cupboard.

She counted her special things.

"One ostrich egg.

Two wishbones.

Three lizard fangs.

Four snake skins."

She lined them up and
shined them up.

Whoosh, came a sound from the sky.

"What is that?" asked Constance.

"Trouble," said Myrna.

They looked out the window.

"Oh no!" yelled Constance.

"They're going to crash!"

But Drusilla and Hiss
did not crash.

They flew right through the window!
That was the good news.
The bad news was that they sucked up
all of Constance's special things!
"WHAT is THAT?" asked Constance.

"Is that any way to say hello?"
asked Drusilla.

"Hello," said Constance.

"There! Now WHAT is THAT?"

15

"THAT is my vacuum," said Drusilla.

"What's the matter with your broom?"
asked Constance.

"I traded it in," said Drusilla.

"I wanted to go to
the country fair in style."

"But it ate up my special things!"
said Constance.

Constance and Myrna looked
at Hiss's tail.

They looked at the vacuum.

"It ate up Hiss's tail too,"
Constance added.

"Double trouble," said Myrna.

"We will not go to the fair
in style," said Constance.

"We will go to the fair the way
we always go to the fair.
We will go on my broom."
"You must go for a ride
before you decide,"
said Drusilla.
Constance shook her head.
Her pointy hat wagged
back and forth.
"I can't," said Constance.
"Why not?" asked Drusilla.
"Because first I must clean
the cottage," said Constance.
"That is not a problem,"
said Drusilla.

Whoosh, went her vacuum.

Goodbye dust!

Goodbye cobwebs!

Goodbye spider eggs!

Constance looked around.

The cottage was really clean!

That was the good news.

The bad news was that the vacuum

had eaten another tail.

Myrna's!

3.
READY, SET, PRACTICE

"Now we must get ready
for the fair," said Drusilla.
"I AM ready for the fair,"
said Constance.
Constance took out her broom.
Drusilla put it back.
"This will be the best year ever,"
said Drusilla.

"Because this year we
will enter the contests.
You and I will win a prize."
Constance shook her head.
"I do not want to enter
a contest," said Constance.
"I am not the fastest.
I am not the strongest.
I am not the smartest.
Because of me we will not win."
"Then we will practice,"
said Drusilla.
"First we will practice for
the sack race."

21

"We cannot practice for
the sack race," said Constance.
"We do not have a sack!"
"That is not a problem,"
said Drusilla.
Drusilla took the pillowcase
off her pillow.

She took the flour out
of its sack.

She drew two lines on the floor.

"Line up!" said Drusilla.

They each put one leg in a sack.

Drusilla lined up with Constance.

Hiss lined up with Myrna.

"Ready, set, go!"

yelled Drusilla.

They thumped.

They jumped.

They bumped.

They all ended up at the finish line!

That was the good news.

The bad news was that they
all ended up in a heap!
"Did we win?" asked Constance.
They looked at each other.
"I think it was a tie,"
said Drusilla.
They laughed and laughed.

"You see," said Constance,
"we will NOT win the sack race."
"Then we will win another contest,"
said Drusilla.
"We will practice for the
greased pig contest," she said.
"WHAT is THAT?" asked Constance.
"It is a contest where you try
to catch a greased pig," said Drusilla.

26

"We cannot practice for the
greased pig contest," said Constance.
"We do not have a pig!"
"That is not a problem," said Drusilla.
She took out the grease.
"We'll pretend that YOU are the pig,"
said Drusilla.
"I'll grease you up and
try to catch you."

Constance shook her head.

"No way!" said Constance.

"YOU can be the pig and I'll
try to catch YOU."

"Let's take turns," said Drusilla.

Drusilla and Constance got greased up.

"Ready, set, go!" said Drusilla.

They slid.

They slipped.

They flopped.

They flipped.

"Bet you can't catch me!" they yelled.

Hiss and Myrna joined in.

They went sliding.

They went gliding.

"Hiss!" said Hiss.

"Oink!" said Myrna.

Drusilla grabbed hold of
something greasy.

Constance grabbed hold of
something greasy.

That was the good news.

The bad news was that they
couldn't hold on.
They all ended up in a heap!
"Butterfingers!" yelled Drusilla.
They laughed and laughed!

"You see," said Constance,
"we will NOT win the
greased pig contest!"
"Then we will win another contest,"
said Drusilla.

Drusilla sat down to think.

She thought so long, she fell asleep.

She tossed and she turned.

She snuffled and she snored.

"I think Drusilla is practicing

for a snoring contest," said Constance.

"And if there WERE a snoring contest,

I think she would win!"

4.
COUNTRY FAIR, AND BACK AGAIN

Constance looked around.

Her cottage was not clean anymore.

Myrna and Hiss were not
clean anymore.

Constance put Myrna and Hiss
in the tub.

Hiss splished.

Myrna splashed.

Drusilla snored.

Constance started cleaning.

Whoosh! went the vacuum.

Drusilla woke up.

"I see you like my vacuum
after all," she said.

"Now it is time to go for a ride.
We will ride to the
fair in style."

"A vacuum is for cleaning,"
Constance said.

"A broom is for riding."

But where was her broom?

It was hidden in the mess.

"Oh no!" said Constance.
"I guess we will have to
take the vacuum," said Drusilla.

Drusilla jumped on.

Constance plopped on behind Drusilla.

The wet pets hopped on
behind Constance.

Off they went out the window!

"Hold on to your hats!"

shouted Drusilla.

"Not so fast!" yelled Constance.

Higher and higher they flew.

They flew over the fair.

They saw the sack contest.

They saw the greased pig contest.

They saw a pie-eating contest.

"Stop!" yelled Constance.

"THAT is a contest I could win!"

she said.

"I am not the fastest.

I am not the strongest.

I am not the smartest.

But I AM the hungriest!"

They flew down.

They ate and ate.

One pie, two pies, three pies, four pies.

They were winning the contest!

"Yum," said Myrna.

All of a sudden Drusilla
stopped eating.
"AHHHHH!" she said.
She looked very green.
Constance stopped eating.
"I think Drusilla is sick!"
said Constance.
"We must take her home!"

Constance picked Drusilla up.

She put Drusilla behind her

on the vacuum.

Myrna and Hiss hopped on.

Constance started up the vacuum.

Whoosh, went the vacuum.

Off they flew.

Whoosh, went the fresh air
on Drusilla's face.
The air made Drusilla feel better.
"Because of me we did not win the contest,"
said Drusilla.
She shook her head sadly.
Her pointy hat wagged back and forth.

Constance smiled.

"That is not a problem," she said.

"There is always next year."

"You are not the fastest," said Drusilla.

"You are not the strongest.

And you may not be the smartest.

But you ARE the nicest!"

"Thank you, Cousin," said Constance.

Higher and higher they flew.

"Hold on to your hats!" shouted Constance.

They held on tight.

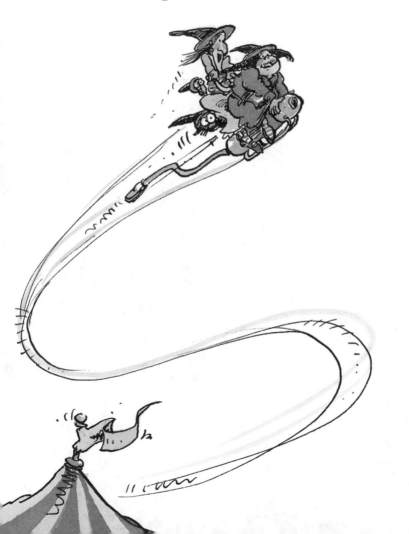

They flew over the fair.

They flew over the foodstand.

They flew over the bandstand.

They flew over the grandstand.

That was the good news.

The bad news was that they sucked up
everything in their path!
And they laughed, and they laughed,
and they laughed!

47

Barbara Mariconda was born and raised in Connecticut, where she lives with her husband, two children, and one very large poodle. In addition to writing, she enjoys teaching second grade, singing, and traveling.

Jon McIntosh has been an illustrator and designer for the past twenty-five years. He lives on the island of Martha's Vineyard.